we Are FAMILY!

Adapted by Sheila Sweeny Higginson
Illustrated by Miles Thompson

Ready-to-Read

Simon Spotlight

New York   London   Toronto   Sydney   New Delhi

SIMON SPOTLIGHT
An imprint of Simon & Schuster Children's Publishing Division
1230 Avenue of the Americas, New York, New York 10020
This Simon Spotlight edition August 2015
TM & © 2015 Sony Pictures Animation Inc. All Rights Reserved.
All rights reserved, including the right of reproduction in whole or in part in any form.
SIMON SPOTLIGHT and colophon are registered trademarks of Simon & Schuster, Inc.
For information about special discounts for bulk purchases, please contact Simon & Schuster
Special Sales at 1-866-506-1949 or business@simonandschuster.com.
Manufactured in the United States of America 0715 LAK
2 4 6 8 10 9 7 5 3 1
ISBN 978-1-4814-4800-0 (hc)
ISBN 978-1-4814-4799-7 (pbk)
ISBN 978-1-4814-4801-7 (eBook)

It's a boy!
(Or is it a vampire?)

Dennis (Denisovich)
Transylvania General Hospital

Dracula loves his new grandson.
He wants his family to be happy.
He gives Johnny a job.
He has the entire hotel
babyproofed for Dennis.

Dracula watches as Dennis grows . . .
and grows . . .

and grows. . . .

He waits for Dennis to grow fangs.
But there is not a pointy tooth
anywhere.

Mavis worries that Transylvania
is not the best place to raise
Dennis. He does not seem to be a
monster—or a vampire—after all.
"We are thinking about moving,"
she tells her father.
She plans a trip with Johnny to
visit his hometown.

"This cannot be happening!
I cannot lose the only family I have!"
Dracula cries.

Mavis is excited to see Santa Cruz!
"I love it here!" she gushes.
"What an awesome place
to raise our child."

Johnny's parents are excited too.
"Our castle is your castle,"
Johnny's mom, Linda, says. "Just
not as spooky."
She decorated the guest room so
Mavis will feel right at home.
Instead, she just feels weird.

While Johnny and Mavis are away,
Dracula babysits Dennis.
He wants him to turn into a vampire
while his parents are gone.

"It's time for me to show Dennis how to be a vampire," Dracula tells his buddies.

They jump into the hearse and head to Camp Winnepacaca.

Camp Winnepacaca has changed
a lot since Dracula was a boy.
All the little vampires are being
nice to one another!
"Remember, a vampire always
shares!" the camp director says.

Dracula can't believe his ears.
Then the campers start to sing,
"Vampires will be friends forever,
through the centuries together."
"What happened to all the good,
scary stuff?" Dracula says with a
huff.

Dracula climbs up the diving tower.
"Denisovich, this is where I learned
to fly!" he says.
"I want to fly!" Dennis cheers.
"Here . . . we . . . go!" Dracula yells
as he tosses Dennis off the tower.

Dracula waits for Dennis to start
flying.
"It will happen," he tells Wayne.
It does not.
It is Grandpa to the rescue!

Later, in Santa Cruz, Johnny gets
sent a video from a friend.
It shows a child daredevil falling
from a tower.
"Wait!" Mavis cries.
"Is that Dennis?"
It is!

Mavis calls her father.
"I am coming back to the hotel right now," she tells him.
"And you had better be there, or you are going to be very sorry."

Mavis and Johnny race to the
airport, but there are no quick
flights to Transylvania.
Luckily, Mavis has wings of
her own.

Mavis is mad, and time is running out for Dracula. He will do anything to keep his family together. Dennis has to become a vampire so Mavis and Johnny won't move away and break up the family!

"I think Vlad could help,"
Frankenstein suggests.
Vlad is Dracula's father.
Dracula agrees.
He heads off to his father's cave.
"I cannot believe I am doing this."
Dracula sighs.

Vlad is surprised to see his son. "This is certainly unexpected," Vlad says. "It's only been what, six hundred years or so?"

"It's about my grandson," Dracula explains. "He does not have his fangs yet."

If anyone can scare the fangs out of
Dennis, it's Vlad!
He agrees to do it at Dennis's
birthday party.

Vlad comes to the birthday party for
Dennis.
Kakie the monster is Dennis's
favorite monster.
He is usually very sweet and friendly.
But Vlad turns Kakie into a
scary monster.

"I want all the cake!" Kakie shouts.
Dennis jumps into Dracula's arms.
"I'm scared!" he cries.
Dracula loves Dennis too much to
let Vlad continue.

"How could you let Vlad do that?"
Mavis yells. "Dennis is just not a
monster or a vampire."
Drac agrees. "You're right! It wasn't
worth it. I don't want to lose him!"

Dennis can't listen to them anymore.
He runs away as fast as he can.
"Dennis! Where are you going?" asks
his friend Winnie.
"Come on. Follow me!" he says.

Vlad is angry. "You call this a
family?" he says.
"You are all weak!"

Dracula doesn't care about whether Dennis is a vampire or not. Dracula only cares about Dennis.

Meanwhile, Bela is trying to kidnap
Dennis. Winnie tries to help Dennis
by biting Bela's hand.

Bela pushes Winnie away, and that
makes Dennis mad! He growls just
like Dracula. Then he opens his
mouth and shows his . . . fangs!

Dennis isn't just a vampire.
He's a superhero!
He saved his family!
Even Vlad is impressed.
There is no denying it now.
Human . . . vampire . . . monster . . .
it does not matter at all
when you are a family!